WITH THESE HANDS

WITH THESE HANDS

by C. M. Kornbluth

No self-respecting artist can object to suffering for his art ... but not in a society where art is outdated by technology!

I

Halvorsen waited in the Chancery office while Monsignor Reedy disposed of three persons who had preceded him. He was a little dizzy with hunger and noticed only vaguely that the prelate's secretary was beckoning to him. He started to his feet when the secretary pointedly opened the door to Monsignor Reedy's inner office and stood waiting beside it.

The artist crossed the floor, forgetting that he had leaned his portfolio against his chair, remembered at the door and went back for it, flushing. The secretary looked patient.

"Thanks," Halvorsen murmured to him as the door closed.

There was something wrong with the prelate's manner.

"I've brought the designs for the Stations, Padre," he said, opening the portfolio on the desk.

"Bad news, Roald," said the monsignor. "I know how you've been looking forward to the commission—"

"Somebody else get it?" asked the artist faintly, leaning against the desk. "I thought his eminence definitely decided I had the—"

"It's not that," said the monsignor. "But the Sacred Congregation of Rites this week made a pronouncement on images of devotion. Stereopantograph is to be licit within a diocese at the discretion of the bishop. And his eminence—"

"S.P.G.—slimy imitations," protested Halvorsen. "Real as a plastic eye. No texture. No guts. *You* know that, Padre!" he said accusingly.

"I'm sorry, Roald," said the monsignor. "Your work is better than we'll get from a stereopantograph—to my eyes, at least. But there are other considerations."

4

"Money!" spat the artist.

"Yes, money," the prelate admitted. "His eminence wants to see the St. Xavier U. building program through before he dies. Is that a mortal sin? And there are our schools, our charities, our Venus mission. S.P.G. will mean a considerable saving on procurement and maintenance of devotional images. Even if I could, I would not disagree with his eminence on adopting it as a matter of diocesan policy."

The prelate's eyes fell on the detailed drawings of the Stations of the Cross and lingered.

"Your St. Veronica," he said abstractedly. "Very fine. It suggests one of Caravaggio's care-worn saints to me. I would have liked to see her in the bronze."

"So would I," said Halvorsen hoarsely. "Keep the drawings, Padre." He started for the door.

"But I can't—"

"That's all right."

The artist walked past the secretary blindly and out of the Chancery into Fifth Avenue's spring sunlight. He hoped Monsignor Reedy was enjoying the drawings and was ashamed of himself and sorry for Halvorsen. And he was glad he didn't have to carry the heavy portfolio any more. Everything seemed so heavy lately—chisels, hammer, wooden palette. Maybe the padre would send him something and pretend it was for expenses or an advance, as he had in the past.

Halvorsen's feet carried him up the Avenue. No, there wouldn't be any advances any more. The last steady trickle of income had just been dried up, by an announcement in *Osservatore Romano*. Religious conservatism had carried the church as far as it would go in its ancient role of art patron.

When all Europe was writing on the wonderful new vellum, the church stuck to good old papyrus. When all Europe was writing on the wonderful new paper, the church stuck to good old vellum. When all architects and municipal monument committees and portrait bust clients were patronizing the stereopantograph, the church stuck to good old expensive sculpture. But not any more.

He was passing an S.P.G. salon now, where one of his Tuesday night pupils worked: one of the few men in the classes. Mostly they consisted of lazy, moody, irritable girls. Halvorsen, surprised at himself, entered the salon, walking between asthenic semi-nude stereos executed in transparent plastic that made the skin of his neck and shoulders prickle with gooseflesh.

Slime! he thought. *How can they—*

"May I help—oh, hello, Roald. What brings you here?"

He knew suddenly what had brought him there. "Could you make a little advance on next month's tuition, Lewis? I'm strapped." He took a nervous look around the chamber of horrors, avoiding the man's condescending face.

"I guess so, Roald. Would ten dollars be any help? That'll carry us through to the 25th, right?"

"Fine, right, sure," he said, while he was being unwillingly towed around the place.

"I know you don't think much of S.P.G., but it's quiet now, so this is a good chance to see how we work. I don't say it's Art with a capital A, but you've got to admit it's *an* art, something people like at a price they can afford to pay. Here's where we sit them. Then you run out the feelers to the reference points on the face. You know what they are?"

He heard himself say dryly: "I know what they are. The Egyptian sculptors used them when they carved statues of the pharaohs."

"Yes? I never knew that. There's nothing new under the Sun, is there? But *this* is the heart of the S.P.G." The youngster proudly swung open the door of an electronic device in the wall of the portrait booth. Tubes winked sullenly at Halvorsen.

WITH THESE HANDS

"The esthetikon?" he asked indifferently. He did not feel indifferent, but it would be absurd to show anger, no matter how much he felt it, against a mindless aggregation of circuits that could calculate layouts, criticize and correct pictures for a desired effect—and that had put the artist of design out of a job.

"Yes. The lenses take sixteen profiles, you know, and we set the esthetikon for whatever we want—cute, rugged, sexy, spiritual, brainy, or a combination. It fairs curves from profile to profile to give us just what we want, distorts the profiles themselves within limits if it has to, and there's your portrait stored in the memory tank waiting to be taped. You set your ratio for any enlargement or reduction you want and play it back. I wish we were reproducing today; it's fascinating to watch. You just pour in your cold-set plastic, the nozzles ooze out a core and start crawling over to scan—a drop here, a worm there, and it begins to take shape.

"We mostly do portrait busts here, the Avenue trade, but Wilgus, the foreman, used to work in a monument shop in Brooklyn. He did that heroic-size war memorial on the East River Drive—hired Garda Bouchette, the TV girl, for the central figure. And what a figure! He told me he set the esthetikon plates for three-quarter sexy, one-quarter spiritual. Here's something interesting—standing figurine of Orin Ryerson, the banker. He ordered twelve. Figurines are coming in. The girls like them because they can show their shapes. You'd be surprised at some of the poses they want to try—"

*

Somehow, Halvorsen got out with the ten dollars, walked to Sixth Avenue and sat down hard in a cheap restaurant. He had coffee and dozed a little, waking with a guilty start at a racket across the street. There was a building going up. For a while he watched the great machines pour walls and floors, the workmen rolling here and there on their little chariots to weld on a wall

7

panel, stripe on an electric circuit of conductive ink, or spray plastic finish over the "wired" wall, all without leaving the saddles of their little mechanical chariots.

Halvorsen felt more determined. He bought a paper from a vending machine by the restaurant door, drew another cup of coffee and turned to the help-wanted ads.

The tricky trade-school ads urged him to learn construction work and make big money. Be a plumbing-machine setup man. Be a house-wiring machine tender. Be a servotruck driver. Be a lumber-stacker operator. Learn pouring-machine maintenance.

Make big money!

A sort of panic overcame him. He ran to the phone booth and dialed a Passaic number. He heard the *ring-ring-ring* and strained to hear old Mr. Krehbeil's stumping footsteps growing louder as he neared the phone, even though he knew he would hear nothing until the receiver was picked up.

*

Ring—ring—ring. "Hello?" grunted the old man's voice, and his face appeared on the little screen. "Hello, Mr. Halvorsen. What can I do for you?"

Halvorsen was tongue-tied. He couldn't possibly say: I just wanted to see if you were still there. I was afraid you weren't there any more. He choked and improvised: "Hello, Mr. Krehbeil. It's about the banister on the stairs in my place. I noticed it's pretty shaky. Could you come over sometime and fix it for me?"

Krehbeil peered suspiciously out of the screen. "I could do that," he said slowly. "I don't have much work nowadays. But you can carpenter as good as me, Mr. Halvorsen, and frankly you're very slow pay and I like cabinet work better. I'm not a young man and climbing around on ladders takes it out of me. If you can't find anybody else, I'll take the work, but I got to have some of the money first, just for the materials. It isn't easy to get good wood any more."

"All right," said Halvorsen. "Thanks, Mr. Krehbeil. I'll call you if I can't get anybody else."

He hung up and went back to his table and newspaper. His face was burning with anger at the old man's reluctance and his own foolish panic. Krehbeil didn't realize they were both in the same leaky boat. Krehbeil, who didn't get a job in a month, still thought with senile pride that he was a journeyman carpenter and cabinetmaker who could make his solid way anywhere with his tool-box and his skill, and that he could afford to look down on anything as disreputable as an artist—even an artist who could carpenter as well as he did himself.

Labuerre had made Halvorsen learn carpentry, and Labuerre had been right. You build a scaffold so you can sculp up high, not so it will collapse and you break a leg. You build your platforms so they hold the rock steady, not so it wobbles and chatters at every blow of the chisel. You build your armatures so they hold the plasticine you slam onto them.

But the help-wanted ads wanted no builders of scaffolds, platforms and armatures. The factories were calling for setup men and maintenance men for the production and assembly machines.

From upstate, General Vegetables had sent a recruiting team for farm help—harvest setup and maintenance men, a few openings for experienced operators of tank-caulking machinery. Under "office and professional" the demand was heavy for computer men, for girls who could run the I.B.M. Letteriter, esp. familiar sales and collections corresp., for office machinery maintenance and repair men. A job printing house wanted an esthetikon operator for letterhead layouts and the like. A.T. & T. wanted trainees to earn while learning telephone maintenance. A direct-mail advertising outfit wanted an artist—no, they wanted a sales-executive who could scrawl picture-ideas that would be subjected to the criticism and correction of the esthetikon.

Halvorsen leafed tiredly through the rest of the paper. He knew he wouldn't get a job, and if he did he wouldn't hold it. He knew it was a terrible thing to admit to yourself that you might starve to death because you were bored by anything except art, but he admitted it.

It had happened often enough in the past—artists undergoing preposterous hardships, not, as people thought, because they were devoted to art, but because nothing else was interesting. If there were only some impressive, sonorous word that summed up the aching, oppressive futility that overcame him when he tried to get out of art—only there wasn't.

He thought he could tell which of the photos in the tabloid had been corrected by the esthetikon.

There was a shot of Jink Bitsy, who was to star in a remake of *Peter Pan.* Her ears had been made to look not pointed but pointy, her upper lip had been lengthened a trifle, her nose had been pugged a little and tilted quite a lot, her freckles were cuter than cute, her brows were innocently arched, and her lower lip and eyes were nothing less than pornography.

There was a shot, apparently uncorrected, of the last Venus ship coming in at La Guardia and the average-looking explorers grinning. Caption: "Austin Malone and crew smile relief on safe arrival. Malone says Venus colonies need men, machines. See story p. 2."

Petulantly, Halvorsen threw the paper under the table and walked out. What had space travel to do with him? Vacations on the Moon and expeditions to Venus and Mars were part of the deadly encroachment on his livelihood and no more.

II

He took the subway to Passaic and walked down a long-still traffic beltway to his studio, almost the only building alive in the slums near the rusting railroad freightyard.

A sign that had once said "F. Labuerre, Sculptor—Portraits and Architectural Commissions" now said "Roald Halvorsen; Art Classes—Reasonable Fees." It was a grimy two-story frame building with a shopfront in which were mounted some of his students' charcoal figure studies and oil still-lifes. He lived upstairs, taught downstairs front, and did his own work downstairs, back behind dirty, ceiling-high drapes.

Going in, he noticed that he had forgotten to lock the door again. He slammed it bitterly. At the noise, somebody called from behind the drapes: "Who's that?"

"Halvorsen!" he yelled in a sudden fury. "I live here. I own this place. Come out of there! What do you want?"

There was a fumbling at the drapes and a girl stepped between them, shrinking from their dirt.

"Your door was open," she said firmly, "and it's a shop. I've just been here a couple of minutes. I came to ask about classes, but I don't think I'm interested if you're this bad-tempered."

A pupil. Pupils were never to be abused, especially not now.

"I'm terribly sorry," he said. "I had a trying day in the city." Now turn it on. "I wouldn't tell everybody a terrible secret like this, but I've lost a commission. You understand? I thought so. Anybody who'd traipse out here to my dingy abode would be *simpatica*. Won't you sit down? No, not there—humor an artist and sit over there. The warm background of that still-life brings out your color—quite good color. Have you ever been painted? You've a very interesting face, you know. Some day I'd like to—but you mentioned classes.

"We have figure classes, male and female models alternating, on Tuesday nights. For that I have to be very stern and ask you to sign up for an entire course of twelve lessons at sixty dollars.

11

It's the models' fees—they're exorbitant. Saturday afternoons we have still-life classes for beginners in oils. That's only two dollars a class, but you might sign up for a series of six and pay ten dollars in advance, which saves you two whole dollars. I also give private instructions to a few talented amateurs."

The price was open on that one—whatever the traffic would bear. It had been a year since he'd had a private pupil and she'd taken only six lessons at five dollars an hour.

"The still-life sounds interesting," said the girl, holding her head self-consciously the way they all did when he gave them the patter. It was a good head, carried well up. The muscles clung close, not yet slacked into geotropic loops and lumps. The line of youth is heliotropic, he confusedly thought. "I saw some interesting things back there. Was that your own work?"

She rose, obviously with the expectation of being taken into the studio. Her body was one of those long-lined, small-breasted, coltish jobs that the pre-Raphaelites loved to draw.

"Well—" said Halvorsen. A deliberate show of reluctance and then a bright smile of confidence. "*You'll* understand," he said positively and drew aside the curtains.

"What a curious place!" She wandered about, inspecting the drums of plaster, clay and plasticene, the racks of tools, the stands, the stones, the chisels, the forge, the kiln, the lumber, the glaze bench.

"I *like* this," she said determinedly, picking up a figure a half-meter tall, a Venus he had cast in bronze while studying under Labuerre some years ago. "How much is it?"

An honest answer would scare her off, and there was no chance in the world that she'd buy. "I hardly ever put my things up for sale," he told her lightly. "That was just a little study. I do work on commission only nowadays."

Her eyes flicked about the dingy room, seeming to take in its scaling plaster and warped floor and see through the wall to the abandoned slum in which it was set. There was amusement in her glance.

I am not being honest, she thinks. She thinks that is funny. Very well, I will be honest. "Six hundred dollars," he said flatly.

*

The girl set the figurine on its stand with a rap and said, half angry and half amused: "I don't understand it. That's more than a month's pay for me. I could get an S.P.G. statuette just as pretty as this for ten dollars. Who do you artists think you are, anyway?"

Halvorsen debated with himself about what he could say in reply:

An S.P.G. operator spends a week learning his skill and I spend a lifetime learning mine.

An S.P.G. operator makes a mechanical copy of a human form distorted by formulae mechanically arrived at from psychotests of population samples. I take full responsibility for my work; it is mine, though I use what I see fit from Egypt, Greece, Rome, the Middle Ages, the Renaissance, the Augustan and Romantic and Modern Eras.

An S.P.G. operator works in soft, homogeneous plastic; I work in bronze that is more complicated than you dream, that is cast and acid-dipped today so it will slowly take on rich and subtle coloring many years from today.

An S.P.G. operator could not make an Orpheus Fountain—

He mumbled, "Orpheus," and keeled over.

*

Halvorsen awoke in his bed on the second floor of the building. His fingers and toes buzzed electrically and he felt very clear-headed. The girl and a man, unmistakably a doctor, were watching him.

"You don't seem to belong to any Medical Plans, Halvorsen," the doctor said irritably. "There weren't any cards on you at all.

No Red, no Blue, no Green, no Brown."

"I used to be on the Green Plan, but I let it lapse," the artist said defensively.

"And look what happened!"

"Stop nagging him!" the girl said. "I'll pay you your fee."

"It's supposed to come through a Plan," the doctor fretted.

"We won't tell anybody," the girl promised. "Here's five dollars. Just stop nagging him."

"Malnutrition," said the doctor. "Normally I'd send him to a hospital, but I don't see how I could manage it. He isn't on any Plan at all. Look, I'll take the money and leave some vitamins. That's what he needs—vitamins. And food."

"I'll see that he eats," the girl said, and the doctor left.

"How long since you've had anything?" she asked Halvorsen.

"I had some coffee today," he answered, thinking back. "I'd been working on detail drawings for a commission and it fell through. I told you that. It was a shock."

"I'm Lucretia Grumman," she said, and went out.

He dozed until she came back with an armful of groceries.

"It's hard to get around down here," she complained.

"It was Labuerre's studio," he told her defiantly. "He left it to me when he died. Things weren't so rundown in his time. I studied under him; he was one of the last. He had a joke—'They don't really want my stuff, but they're ashamed to let me starve.' He warned me that they wouldn't be ashamed to let *me* starve, but I insisted and he took me in."

Halvorsen drank some milk and ate some bread. He thought of the change from the ten dollars in his pocket and decided not to mention it. Then he remembered that the doctor had gone through his pockets.

"I can pay you for this," he said. "It's very kind of you, but you mustn't think I'm penniless. I've just been too preoccupied to take care of myself."

"Sure," said the girl. "But we can call this an advance. I want to sign up for some classes."

"Be happy to have you."

"Am I bothering you?" asked the girl. "You said something odd when you fainted—'Orpheus.'"

"Did I say that? I must have been thinking of Milles' Orpheus Fountain in Copenhagen. I've seen photos, but I've never been there."

"Germany? But there's nothing left of Germany."

"Copenhagen's in Denmark. There's quite a lot of Denmark left. It was only on the fringes. Heavily radiated, but still there."

"I want to travel, too," she said. "I work at La Guardia and I've never been off, except for an orbiting excursion. I want to go to the Moon on my vacation. They give us a bonus in travel vouchers. It must be wonderful dancing under the low gravity."

Spaceport? Off? Low gravity? Terms belonging to the detested electronic world of the stereopantograph in which he had no place.

"Be very interesting," he said, closing his eyes to conceal disgust.

"I *am* bothering you. I'll go away now, but I'll be back Tuesday night for the class. What time do I come and what should I bring?"

"Eight. It's charcoal—I sell you the sticks and paper. Just bring a smock."

"All right. And I want to take the oils class, too. And I want to bring some people I know to see your work. I'm sure they'll see something they like. Austin Malone's in from Venus—he's a special friend of mine."

"Lucretia," he said. "Or do some people call you Lucy?"

"Lucy."

"Will you take that little bronze you liked? As a thank you?"

"I can't do that!"

"Please. I'd feel much better about this. I really mean it."

She nodded abruptly, flushing, and almost ran from the room.

Now why did I do that? he asked himself. He hoped it was because he liked Lucy Grumman very much. He hoped it wasn't a cold-blooded investment of a piece of sculpture that would never be sold, anyway, just to make sure she'd be back with class fees and more groceries.

III

She was back on Tuesday, a half-hour early and carrying a smock. He introduced her formally to the others as they arrived: a dozen or so bored young women who, he suspected, talked a great deal about their art lessons outside, but in class used any excuse to stop sketching.

He didn't dare show Lucy any particular consideration. There were fierce little miniature cliques in the class. Halvorsen knew they laughed at him and his line among themselves, and yet, strangely, were fiercely jealous of their seniority and right to individual attention.

The lesson was an ordeal, as usual. The model, a muscle-bound young graduate of the barbell gyms and figure-photography studios, was stupid and argumentative about ten-minute poses. Two of the girls came near a hair-pulling brawl over the rights to a preferred sketching location. A third girl had discovered Picasso's cubist period during the past week and proudly announced that she didn't *feel* perspective in art.

But the two interminable hours finally ticked by. He nagged them into cleaning up—not as bad as the Saturdays with oils—and stood by the open door. Otherwise they would have stayed all night, cackling about absent students and snarling sulkily among themselves. His well-laid plans went sour, though. A large and flashy car drove up as the girls were leaving.

"That's Austin Malone," said Lucy. "He came to pick me up

and look at your work."

That was all the wedge her fellow-pupils needed.

"*Aus*-tin Ma-*lone*! *Well!*"

"Lucy, darling, I'd love to meet a real *spaceman*."

"Roald, darling, would you mind very much if I stayed a moment?"

"I'm certainly not going to miss this and I don't care if you mind or not, Roald, darling!"

Malone was an impressive figure. Halvorsen thought: he looks as though he's been run through an esthetikon set for 'brawny' and 'determined.' Lucy made a hash of the introductions and the spaceman didn't rise to conversational bait dangled enticingly by the girls.

In a clear voice, he said to Halvorsen: "I don't want to take up too much of your time. Lucy tells me you have some things for sale. Is there any place we can look at them where it's quiet?"

The students made sulky exits.

"Back here," said the artist.

The girl and Malone followed him through the curtains. The spaceman made a slow circuit of the studio, seeming to repel questions.

He sat down at last and said: "I don't know what to think, Halvorsen. This place stuns me. Do you *know* you're in the Dark Ages?"

People who never have given a thought to Chartres and Mont St. Michel usually call it the Dark Ages, Halvorsen thought wryly. He asked, "Technologically, you mean? No, not at all. My plaster's better, my colors are better, my metal is better—tool metal, not casting metal, that is."

"I mean *hand* work," said the spaceman. "Actually working by *hand*."

The artist shrugged. "There have been crazes for the techniques of the boiler works and the machine shop," he admitted. "Some interesting things were done, but they didn't stand up well. Is there anything here that takes your eye?"

"I like those dolphins," said the spaceman, pointing to a perforated terra-cotta relief on the wall. They had been commissioned by an architect, then later refused for reasons of economy when the house had run way over estimate. "They'd look bully over the fireplace in my town apartment. Like them, Lucy?"

"I think they're wonderful," said the girl.

Roald saw the spaceman go rigid with the effort not to turn and stare at her. He loved her and he was jealous.

Roald told the story of the dolphins and said: "The price that the architect thought was too high was three hundred and sixty dollars."

Malone grunted. "Doesn't seem unreasonable—if you set a high store on inspiration."

"I don't know about inspiration," the artist said evenly. "But I was awake for two days and two nights shoveling coal and adjusting drafts to fire that thing in my kiln."

The spaceman looked contemptuous. "I'll take it," he said. "Be something to talk about during those awkward pauses. Tell me, Halvorsen, how's Lucy's work? Do you think she ought to stick with it?"

"Austin," objected the girl, "don't be so blunt. How can he possibly know after one day?"

"She can't draw yet," the artist said cautiously. "It's all coordination, you know—thousands of hours of practice, training your eye and hand to work together until you can put a line on paper where you want it. Lucy, if you're really interested in it, you'll learn to draw well. I don't think any of the other students will. They're in it because of boredom or snobbery, and they'll stop before they have their eye-hand coordination."

"I *am* interested," she said firmly.

Malone's determined restraint broke. "Damned right you are. In—" He recovered himself and demanded of Halvorsen: "I understand your point about coordination. But thousands of hours when you can buy a camera? It's absurd."

"I was talking about drawing, not art," replied Halvorsen. "Drawing is putting a line on paper where you want it, I said." He took a deep breath and hoped the great distinction wouldn't sound ludicrous and trivial. "So let's say that art is knowing how to put the line in the right place."

"Be practical. There isn't any art. Not any more. I get around quite a bit and I never see anything but photos and S.P.G.s. A few heirlooms, yes, but nobody's painting or carving any more."

"There's some art, Malone. My students—a couple of them in the still-life class—are quite good. There are more across the country. Art for occupational therapy, or a hobby, or something to do with the hands. There's trade in their work. They sell them to each other, they give them to their friends, they hang them on their walls. There are even some sculptors like that. Sculpture is prescribed by doctors. The occupational therapists say it's even better than drawing and painting, so some of these people work in plasticene and soft stone, and some of them get to be good."

"Maybe so. I'm an engineer, Halvorsen. We glory in doing things the easy way. Doing things the easy way got me to Mars and Venus and it's going to get me to Ganymede. You're doing things the hard way, and your inefficiency has no place in this world. Look at you! You've lost a fingertip—some accident, I suppose."

"I never noticed—" said Lucy, and then let out a faint, "Oh!"

Halvorsen curled the middle finger of his left hand into the palm, where he usually carried it to hide the missing first joint.

"Yes," he said softly. "An accident."

19

"Accidents are a sign of inadequate mastery of material and equipment," said Malone sententiously. "While you stick to your methods and I stick to mine, *you can't compete with me.*"

His tone made it clear that he was talking about more than engineering.

"Shall we go now, Lucy? Here's my card, Halvorsen. Send those dolphins along and I'll mail you a check."

IV

The artist walked the half-dozen blocks to Mr. Krehbeil's place the next day. He found the old man in the basement shop of his fussy house, hunched over his bench with a powerful light overhead. He was trying to file a saw.

"Mr. Krehbeil!" Halvorsen called over the shriek of metal.

The carpenter turned around and peered with watery eyes. "I can't see like I used to," he said querulously. "I go over the same teeth on this damn saw, I skip teeth, I can't see the light shine off it when I got one set. The glare." He banged down his three-cornered file petulantly. "Well, what can I do for you?"

"I need some crating stock. Anything. I'll trade you a couple of my maple four-by-fours."

The old face became cunning. "And will you set my saw? My *saws*, I mean. It's nothing to you—an hour's work. You have the eyes."

Halvorsen said bitterly, "All right." The old man had to drive his bargain, even though he might never use his saws again. And then the artist promptly repented of his bitterness, offering up a quick prayer that his own failure to conform didn't make him as much of a nuisance to the world as Krehbeil was.

The carpenter was pleased as they went through his small stock of wood and chose boards to crate the dolphin relief. He was pleased enough to give Halvorsen coffee and cake before the artist buckled down to filing the saws.

20

Over the kitchen table, Halvorsen tried to probe. "Things pretty slow now?"

It would be hard to spoil Krehbeil's day now. "People are always fools. They don't know good hand work. Some day," he said apocalyptically, "I laugh on the other side of my face when their foolish machine-buildings go falling down in a strong wind, all of them, all over the country. Even my boy—I used to beat him good, almost every day—he works a foolish concrete machine and his house should fall on his head like the rest."

Halvorsen knew it was Krehbeil's son who supported him by mail, and changed the subject. "You get some cabinet work?"

"Stupid women! What they call antiques—they don't know Meissen, they don't know Biedermeier. They bring me trash to repair sometimes. I make them pay; I swindle them good."

"I wonder if things would be different if there were anything left over in Europe...."

"People will still be fools, Mr. Halvorsen," said the carpenter positively. "Didn't you say you were going to file those saws today?"

So the artist spent two noisy hours filing before he carried his crating stock to the studio.

*

Lucy was there. She had brought some things to eat. He dumped the lumber with a bang and demanded: "Why aren't you at work?"

"We get days off," she said vaguely. "Austin thought he'd give me the cash for the terra-cotta and I could give it to you."

She held out an envelope while he studied her silently. The farce was beginning again. But this time he dreaded it.

It would not be the first time that a lonesome, discontented girl chose to see him as a combination of romantic rebel and lost pup, with the consequences you'd expect.

He knew from books, experience and Labuerre's conversation

in the old days that there was nothing novel about the comedy—that there had even been artists, lots of them, who had counted on endless repetitions of it for their livelihood.

The girl drops in with groceries and the artist is pleasantly surprised; the girl admires this little thing or that after payday and buys it and the artist is pleasantly surprised; the girl brings her friends to take lessons or make little purchases and the artist is pleasantly surprised. The girl may be seduced by the artist or vice versa, which shortens the comedy, or they get married, which lengthens it somewhat.

It had been three years since Halvorsen had last played out the farce with a manic-depressive divorcee from Elmira: three years during which he had crossed the mid-point between thirty and forty; three more years to get beaten down by being unwanted and working too much and eating too little.

Also, he knew, he was in love with this girl.

He took the envelope, counted three hundred and twenty dollars and crammed it into his pocket. "That was your idea," he said. "Thanks. Now get out, will you? I've got work to do."

She stood there, shocked.

"*I said get out. I have work to do.*"

"Austin was right," she told him miserably. "You don't care how people feel. You just want to get things out of them."

She ran from the studio, and Halvorsen fought with himself not to run after her.

He walked slowly into his workshop and studied his array of tools, though he paid little attention to his finished pieces. It would be nice to spend about half of this money on open-hearth steel rod and bar stock to forge into chisels; he thought he knew where he could get some—but she would be back, or he would break and go to her and be forgiven and the comedy would be played out, after all.

He couldn't let that happen.

WITH THESE HANDS

V

Aalesund, on the Atlantic side of the Dourefeld mountains of Norway, was in the lee of the blasted continent. One more archeologist there made no difference, as long as he had the sense to recognize the propellor-like international signposts that said with their three blades, *Radiation Hazard*, and knew what every schoolboy knew about protective clothing and reading a personal Geiger counter.

The car Halvorsen rented was for a brief trip over the mountains to study contaminated Oslo. Well-muffled, he could make it and back in a dozen hours and no harm done.

But he took the car past Oslo, Wennersborg and Goteborg, along the Kattegat coast to Helsingborg, and abandoned it there, among the three-bladed polyglot signs, crossing to Denmark. Danes were as unlike Prussians as they could be, but their unfortunate little peninsula was a sprout off Prussia which radio-cobalt dust couldn't tell from the real thing. The three-bladed signs were most specific.

With a long way to walk along the rubble-littered highways, he stripped off the impregnated coveralls and boots. He had long since shed the noisy counter and the uncomfortable gloves and mask.

The silence was eerie as he limped into Copenhagen at noon. He didn't know whether the radiation was getting to him or whether he was tired and hungry and no more. As though thinking of a stranger, he liked what he was doing.

I'll be my own audience, he thought. God knows I learned there isn't any other, not any more. You have to know when to stop. Rodin, the dirty old, wonderful old man, knew that. He taught us not to slick it and polish it and smooth it until it looked like liquid instead of bronze and stone. Van Gogh was crazy as a loon, but he knew when to stop and varnish it, and he didn't care if the paint looked like

23

paint instead of looking like sunset clouds or moonbeams. Up in Hartford, Browne and Sharpe stop when they've got a turret lathe; they don't put caryatids on it. I'll stop while my life is a life, before it becomes a thing with distracting embellishments such as a wife who will come to despise me, a succession of gradually less worthwhile pieces that nobody will look at.

Blame nobody, he told himself, lightheadedly.

And then it was in front of him, terminating a vista of weeds and bomb rubble—Milles' Orpheus Fountain.

It took a man, he thought. Esthetikon circuits couldn't do it. There was a gross mixture of styles, a calculated flaw that the esthetikon couldn't be set to make. Orpheus and the souls were classic or later; the three-headed dog was archaic. That was to tell you about the antiquity and invincibility of Hell, and that Cerberus knows Orpheus will never go back into life with his bride.

There was the heroic, tragic central figure that looked mighty enough to battle with the gods, but battle wasn't any good against the grinning, knowing, hateful three-headed dog it stood on. You don't battle the pavement where you walk or the floor of the house you're in; you can't. So Orpheus, his face a mask of controlled and suffering fury crashes a great chord from his lyre that moved trees and stones. Around him the naked souls in Hell start at the chord, each in its own way: the young lovers down in death; the mother down in death; the musician, deaf and down in death, straining to hear.

Halvorsen, walking uncertainly toward the fountain, felt something break inside him, and a heaviness in his lungs. As he pitched forward among the weeds, he thought he heard the chord from the lyre and didn't care that the three-headed dog was grinning its knowing, hateful grin down at him.

VI

WITH THESE HANDS

When Halvorsen awoke, he supposed he was in Hell. There were the young lovers, arms about each other's waists, solemnly looking down at him, and the mother was placidly smoothing his brow. He stirred and felt his left arm fall heavily.

"Ah," said the mother, "you mustn't." He felt her pick up his limp arm and lay it across his chest. "Your poor finger!" she sighed. "Can you talk? What happened to it?"

He could talk, weakly. "Labuerre and I," he said. "We were moving a big block of marble with the crane—somehow the finger got under it. I didn't notice until it was too late to shift my grip without the marble slipping and smashing on the floor."

The boy said in a solemn, adolescent croak: "You mean you saved the marble and lost your finger?"

"Marble," he muttered. "It's so hard to get. Labuerre was so old."

The young lovers exchanged a glance and he slept again. He was half awake when the musician seized first one of his hands and then the other, jabbing them with stubby fingers and bending his lion's head close to peer at the horny callouses left by chisel and mallet.

"*Ja, ja*," the musician kept saying.

Hell goes on forever, so for an eternity he jolted and jarred, and for an eternity he heard bickering voices: "Why he was so foolish, then?" "A idiot he could be." "Hush, let him rest." "The children told the story." "There only one Labuerre was." "Easy with the tubing." "Let him rest."

Daylight dazzled his eyes.

"Why you were so foolish?" demanded a harsh voice. "The sister says I can talk to you now, so that is what I first want to know."

He looked at the face of—not the musician; that had been delirium. But it was a tough old face.

25

"*Ja*, I am mean-looking; that is settled. What did you think you were doing without coveralls and way over your exposure time?"

"I wanted to die," said Halvorsen. There were tubes sticking in his arms.

The crag-faced old man let out a contemptuous bellow.

"Sister!" he shouted. "Pull the plasma tubes out before more we waste. He says he wants to die."

"Hush," said the nurse. She laid her hand on his brow again.

"Don't bother with him, Sister," the old man jeered. "He is a shrinking little flower, too delicate for the great, rough world. He has done nothing, he can do nothing, so he decides to make of himself a nuisance by dying."

"You lie," said Halvorsen. "I worked. Good God, how I worked! Nobody wanted my work. They wanted me, to wear in their buttonholes like a flower. They were getting to me. Another year and I wouldn't have been an artist any more."

"*Ja?*" asked the old man. "Tell me about it."

Halvorsen told him, sometimes weeping with self-pity and weakness, sometimes cursing the old man for not letting him die, sometimes quietly describing this statuette or that portrait head, or raving wildly against the mad folly of the world.

At the last he told the old man about Lucy.

"You cannot have everything, you know," said his listener.

"I can have her," answered the artist harshly. "You wouldn't let me die, so I won't die. I'll go back and I'll take her away from that fat-head Malone that she ought to marry. I'll give her a couple of happy years working herself to skin and bones for me before she begins to hate it—before I begin to hate it."

"You can't go back," said the old man. "I'm Cerberus. You understand that? The girl is nothing. The society you come from is nothing. We have a place here.... Sister, can he sit up?"

The woman smiled and cranked his bed. Halvorsen saw

through a picture window that he was in a mountain-rimmed valley that was very green and dotted with herds and unpainted houses.

"Such a place there had to be," said the old man. "In the whole geography of Europe, there had to be a Soltau Valley with winds and terrain just right to deflect the dust."

"Nobody knows?" whispered the artist.

"We prefer it that way. It's impossible to get some things, but you would be surprised how little difference it makes to the young people. They are great travelers, the young people, in their sweaty coveralls with radiation meters. They think when they see the ruined cities that the people who lived in them must have been mad. It was a little travel party like that which found you. The boy was impressed by something you said, and I saw some interesting things in your hands. There isn't much rock around here; we have fine deep topsoil. But the boys could get you stone.

"There should be a statue of the Mayor for one thing, before I die. And from the Rathaus the wooden angels have mostly broken off. Soltau Valley used to be proud of them—could you make good copies? And of course cameras are useless and the best drawings we can do look funny. Could you teach the youngers at least to draw so faces look like faces and not behinds? And like you were saying about you and Labuerre, maybe one younger there will be so crazy that he will want to learn it all, so Soltau will always have an artist and sculptor for the necessary work. And you will find a Lucy or somebody better. I think better."

"Hush," warned the nurse. "You're exciting the patient."

"It's all right," said Halvorsen eagerly. "Thanks, but it's really all right."

www.ingramcontent.com/pod-product-compliance
Lightning Source LLC
Chambersburg PA
CBHW050921120626
46552CB00004B/1685